14 Days

3 2001

MAY   7 2001

AN 3 0 1995   JULY   6 2002

995

994

Letters from Calico Cat

written and illustrated by Donald Charles

CHILDRENS PRESS, CHICAGO

for my mother

Charles, Donald.
   Letters from Calico Cat.

   SUMMARY: Calico Coat shows the reader the letters of
the alphabet.
   [1. Alphabet books] I. Title.
PZ7.C374Le   [E]   74-8181
ISBN 0-516-03519-3

10 11 12 R 87 86 85 84

Letters from Calico Cat

Aa

awake

Bb
butterfly

Cc

cricket

Dd

dance

Ee

eye

Ff

flower

Gg

goldfish

Hh

hungry

Ii

ivy

J j

jay

13

Kk

kite

L l

ladder

Mm

mouse

16

Nn

nose

Oo
owl

Pp
pumpkin

Qq
quick

Rr

rabbit

Ss

slow

Tt
turtle

j 40814

23

Uu

umbrella

Vv
violets

watermelon

Xx

x-ray

Yy
yawn

Zz

ZZZZZZZZZ

Calico Cat
knows his letters.
Do you?

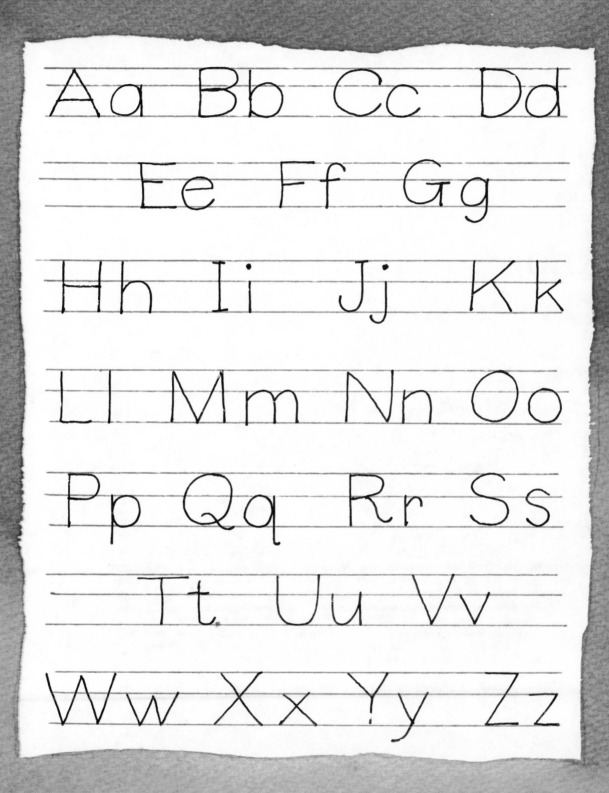

Aa Bb Cc Dd
Ee Ff Gg
Hh Ii Jj Kk
Ll Mm Nn Oo
Pp Qq Rr Ss
Tt Uu Vv
Ww Xx Yy Zz

ABOUT THE AUTHOR/ARTIST

Donald Charles started his long career as an artist and author more than twenty-five years ago after attending the University of California and the Art League School of California. He began by writing and illustrating feature articles for the San Francisco Chronicle, and also sold cartoons and ideas to The New Yorker and Cosmopolitan magazines. Since then he has been at various times, a longshoreman, ranch hand, truck driver, and editor of a weekly newspaper, all enriching experiences for a writer and artist. Ultimately he became creative director for an advertising agency, a post which he resigned several years ago to devote himself full-time to book illustration and writing. Mr. Charles has received frequent awards from graphic societies, and his work has appeared in numerous textbooks and periodicals. He and his artist wife have restored a turn-of-the-century frame house in Chicago where they live with their three children.